The Gingerbread Man

retold by Catherine McCafferty   illustrated by Doug Bowles

School Specialty Publishing

Copyright © 2002 School Specialty Publishing. Published by Brighter Child®,
an imprint of School Specialty Publishing, a member of the School Specialty Family.
Send all inquiries to: School Specialty Publishing, 8720 Orion Place, Columbus, Ohio 43240-2111
Made in the USA.   ISBN 1-57768-368-4   8 9 PHX 11 10 09

 nce upon a time, a kind old couple lived in a land not so far from here. They had all that they wanted, except for a child. Every day in the park, they saw children running and singing. They wished for a child of their own who would run and sing just like the others.

The old woman made up her mind. "If we cannot have a child," she said, "I will make one for us."

That afternoon, the old woman mixed spices
and eggs and flour into a rich dough. She shaped
a gingerbread man and put him on a tray. After
baking the gingerbread man, the old woman trimmed
him with white icing. She took out candy and added a
face and buttons.

What a sweet, perfect child, the old woman thought.

But children are full of surprises, and the Gingerbread Man was no different. He jumped off the tray and began to run, just as the old couple had wished.

But he ran and jumped right out of the window!

The old woman and the old man chased after him.

The Gingerbread Man just ran and sang, "You can run and run as fast as you can! You can't catch me—I'm the Gingerbread Man!"

Before long, a cat saw the Gingerbread Man. *Hmm,* thought the cat, *he will make a tasty meal.*

"Oh, Gingerbread Man," purred the cat, "do stop for a visit."

The Gingerbread Man just ran and sang, "I ran from the old couple, and now I'll run from you. You can run and run as fast as you can. You can't catch me—I'm the Gingerbread Man!"

And so the cat dashed after the old couple, who chased the Gingerbread Man.

A slithering snake soon spied them.
"Sssstop to ssssay hello, Gingerbread Man,"
he hissed.

The Gingerbread Man just ran and sang,

"I ran from the old couple and the cat, and now I'll run from you! You can run and run as fast as you can. You can't catch me—I'm the Gingerbread Man!"

And so the snake slithered after the cat, who dashed after the old couple, who chased the Gingerbread Man.

A great goose saw them next. "I'd be glad to have you for dinner!" he honked to the Gingerbread Man.

The Gingerbread Man just ran and sang,

"I ran from the old couple and the cat and the snake, and now I'll run from you! You can run and run as fast as you can. You can't catch me—I'm the Gingerbread Man!"

And so the goose waddled after the snake, who slithered after the cat, who dashed after the old couple, who chased the Gingerbread Man.

Sly Fox spotted the Gingerbread Man. The fox had a head full of ideas—and a very empty tummy.

The Gingerbread Man saw Fox ahead, but he wasn't worried. He was having too much fun. Fox did not try to stop him, but the Gingerbread Man sang out his song anyway.

"You can't have me for lunch, Fox! I ran from the old couple and the cat and the snake and the goose, and now I'll run from you! You can run and run as fast as you can. You can't catch me—I'm the Gingerbread Man!"

Fox just smiled. "Why would I want to eat you?" he said. "It is much more fun to watch you run. And perhaps I can help you."

"Soon you will come to the river," said Fox. "If you can't cross it, they will catch you."

The Gingerbread Man looked at the water. He knew if he got wet, he would fall apart. "Will you help me cross the water, Fox?" he asked.

"Of course," crafty Fox told him. "I will give you a ride."
The Gingerbread Man hopped on Fox's tail just as the old couple reached for him.

Fox swam away from the shore. "The water will be deep soon," he said. "Climb higher onto my back."

The Gingerbread Man climbed higher, enjoying his fine ride.

Fox stopped in the middle of the river. "The water is getting deeper," he told the Gingerbread Man. "Jump up here, onto my nose."

And so the Gingerbread Man jumped toward Fox's nose. But in the snap of a jaw, he was in Fox's mouth!

Fox smacked his lips and sang a song of his own. "He ran and ran into my clever plan. What a sweet lunch, that Gingerbread Man."